I0537715

BIG HAND

GEORGE COMBE

Copyright © 2017 George Combe

All rights reserved. No part of this book may be reproduced in any manner whatsoever without written consent from the author. This book is a work of fiction and should not be construed as real. The names, characters, places and incidents are products of the author's imagination. Any similarities to person's (living or dead), actual events. Locations and organizations are entirely coincidental.

Full Moon Publishing, LLC
Glade Spring, VA
Fullmoonpublishingllc.com

Cover Design by Danielle Stamper

ISBN: 194623205X
ISBN-13: 978-1946232052

It's good to be near the center of things, where surprises are few and infrequent, where the results of ruminations launched down time's inconstant corridors can be seen coming a long way off. And yet...predictability only masks waiting dissolution for so long, a problem, black holes were developed to address.

Now, a handful of malcontents protest. The cure may be worse than the disease, they suggest, wishing to tinker with the raft of conditions (long declared lawful) that seed a microbe sized birth in deep-space, destined to gobble solar systems. Warped systems no longer evolving, prey to entropy, and striking discordant tones in the music of the spheres.

There is no disagreement that the accelerated involution of black holes is preferable to the tedious systems of decay that prompted their invention.

A delegation of worry warts petitioned the third great spirit of Elohim. Conditions in two concentrations of our Multiverse suggest, if pattern of expansion and condensation continues unimpeded, will briefly mirror the conditions of a devolving concentration, raising the specter of an unwanted black hole birthing itself.

The third great spirit of Elohim, referred to as Fast Eddie by the other six, due to his speedy decision making, questioned the petitioners.

"Are these two near each other?"

"No, different galaxies."

"Near galactic centers?"

The senior worry wart shook his head. "Both in the boonies."

"Wait," said the great spirit, and turned to confer with his fellow Elohim, leaving the petitioners in a state of grace they would have loved to stay in forever.

"Do any of you fellows know a top flight black hole guy?" he asked the other six.

The fifth great spirit of Elohim replied, "My tenth wife has a great nephew, said to be the most talented tuner in his quadrant. He and his better half ramrod a team that's never had a member sucked into a black hole."

The other Elohim mutter, "Impressive. Hard to believe. Knock on wood."

The black hole tuner's wife possesses gravity far beyond that suggested by her physical mass. She's always been able to make herself heavier, a lot heavier, and she can operate her body perfectly even when she weighs thousands of tons.

She is the reason her husband's group of tuners and ticklers has never lost a member to the overwhelming suck of a finely tuned black hole.

One of their crew exhibits the slight but horrifying acceleration toward the place you don't come back from, she makes herself real heavy, real fast. When her density overthrows the baby black hole's negative mass, the panicked assistant tickler stops waving his arms and kicking his legs, all living tissue within a quarter light-day stops moving, and the assistant tickler shoots through the group at blinding speed, while the chief tuner's wife tries to look amazed, dumping dark matter into the void as fast as she can.

This is the second worker she's saved, but she looks the same at a couple million tons as at one-twenty, so no one suspects. She aims to keep it that way, until whoever made her this way steps forward.

The assistant tickler gets control of his velocity and works his way back to the group, where he gets flak for being so nasty he made a black hole blow chunks.

The black hole tuner and his wife are in a luxurious suite on the seventh level of the dimension traveler, a device developed by the Elohim to bypass the action of time in inter-galactic travel. The pair have bodies of universal plasma, required for the jobs they do, and can assume any physical form, but prefer, whenever possible, to take the forms they were born in, big white poodles with hairy hands instead of paws.

They finish a huge meal of a quality unavailable anywhere but within the dimension traveler, and are now involved in a favorite activity to aid digestion, a form of tag that requires flipping the opponent onto its back to become the pursued. The wife cheats by increasing her weight whenever hubby gets a handhold and tries to flip her, but he doesn't seem to be catching on as she'd hoped.

Great civilizations are born, flourish and decline, while the couple roughhouses inside the motionless seventh dimension segment of the traveler, until the Triune creator's attention touches briefly the remote edge of a distant galaxy, and the frolicking white poodles disappear from their luxurious suite, manifesting instantly where the creator's attention touched.

"Did you feel that?" the husband thought to his wife.

"You know I did, and the only question I'm

interested in answering now is what do I have to do to feel it again?"

"When we resolve this anomaly, the seventh dimension portal will open and we'll be back in our suite."

"Will we get that feeling again?"

"No, it only happens outgoing through three or more galactic layers. If you like it too much you'll be headed for early retirement, like my last wife."

"I thought she left you."

"She did, for a gas giant, where she can indulge the class of sensations we just experienced to her heart's content. But she'll never do useful work again."

"Oh."

"Do you feel the eddy?"

"Now that you mention it, yes. It's very subtle."

"It's out of such subtleties black holes manifest."

"Will there be one here?"

"That's for us to determine, or maybe decide."

They melded together into a uniform sphere,

tuned themselves to the octave of the nearest star, and fell toward it at just under light speed, changing octaves when they passed through the system's cometary layer, letting inertia carry them through the planetary layers.

A signal from a moon of the innermost gas giant arrested their momentum, begged their pardon, and requested permission to confer with them before they proceeded to the system's inner planes.

The almost invisible sphere split down the middle, and the pair of large white poodles appeared, startlingly bright, reflecting emanations of a certain length from the gas giant, storing shorter ones in their bodies.

The black hole tuner's wife thought to him, "Darling, these emanations are wonderful. I could stay here for ages."

"Better than coming out of the dimension traveler?"

"Well...no."

"Please don't let these sensate experiences

touch your emotions. I don't want to lose another wife."

A transpace bubble appeared next to them, and they bled through the portal, adjusting their bodies to the atmosphere within. One of the gas giant's moons grew larger overhead until the reversal occurred and they were descending toward a large white hill protruding out of multi-colored flora and fauna covering the surface of this planet in embryo. The transpace bubble dropped them on the hilltop and disappeared.

Tuner and wife found themselves surrounded by white poodles, sitting at attention, making the entire hill white

"This is weird," said the wife.

"I'd say we're related."

"These are our ancestors?"

"Offspring, more likely."

"But we haven't made any children."

"Looks like we're going to."

"But...but..."

"Don't try to get your mind around it. Our

bosses call themselves Masters of Time, we can only pull our weight and hope like hell they're right."

"There's no way to be sure they came from us," she thought.

"If they were good at flip-tag," thought Hubby, "it would be a strong indicator."

They approached the nearest white poodles, who remained at seated attention, watching with greater attention, as the tuner and his mate came up nose to nose, flipped a pair onto their backs, flipped another pair for good measure and fled, stopping a short distance away to check results. The first two flipped were in hot pursuit, the second pair flipping neighbors and fleeing.

"They know the rules," thought wife.

"Jump high and turn to plasma."

They did, becoming a translucent cloud, drifting higher. Their pursuers ran in circles below.

"Let's give them a religious experience," the tuner thought, "and get on with our mission."

"What do you suggest?"

"We make ourselves look giant size, floating up here. When they're settled down and paying attention, I'll howl three times, like a wolf, and we'll rain the short emanations we've been sandbagging down on them. We can get more on the way out."

"What will the emanations do?"

"The ones who absorb them will get smarter."

"They sent a transpace bubble, how much smarter do you want them to get?"

"The bubble was sent by Mr. Almost a Star, looming behind our heads, or it wouldn't have left after delivering us."

"I'll be darned," thought the wife. "Let me hear those howls, big boy."

The planets, complex living beings, continuously exchanged matter of various densities while orbiting their star, denser exchanges occurring at a leisurely pace, often less than half the speed of light. But riding the more ethereal you could really cook. Tuner and wife got off the stream, turned poodle and took in their surroundings. "Why are we…" the wife thought, "oh, I feel, it's the same anomaly all the way down."

"Good girl. Come here and give me some nuzzle."

"Just slip me some plasma, handsome...Eeek, not that much plasma, nasty boy."

"You know you love it."

"Of course, but give a girl some warning."

They had been dropped into the eddy a couple light days out, in interstellar space, and the tuner's experience told him it would pass through the local star's corona and reach a couple light days beyond.

Experience also told him they were now in the vicinity of its cause.

Nearest and smallest, a planet shaped like an enormous bird of prey atop a desolate mountain, back to them, head in partial profile, the great curving beak bathed in sunlight.

Two others visible beyond, the first lop-sided and off kilter, its atmosphere uneven and oddly colored, the other, more distant, a perfect sphere with mixtures of color and shadow moving within, and a glowing tail of long emanations feeding into the lop-sided monstrosity between itself and the bird shaped planet.

Two tiny but exceedingly bright dots of light appeared on the surface of the great bird's massive beak, and began moving at incredible speed, in expanding concentric circles across its surface.

Finally, the tuner stopped moving at the top of the beak that swept down to a wicked point, below which a stream of short emanations poured into the great bird shaped edifice from the lop-sided planet.

His wife bounded over to him and looked down at the stream of emanations flowing into the great bird.

"It's so beautiful," she said.

"If you can stand the screaming."

"What screaming?"

"Be glad there's not much atmosphere here. Most of this stream is composed of souls, or what's left of the souls of members of the dominant species on that lop-sided planet. Much of what they call their technology consists of finding more efficient ways of destroying one another's existence.

"A certain percentage display unusual talent for subjugating others of their kind, and persuading them to pursue honor and acclaim by slaughtering members of other tribes, who pose no threat, they beguile these simpletons with visions of power and respect they have no intention of sharing, then settle their debt with worthless trinkets presented with great ceremony.

"When death takes them, they have nothing left in them of value to the lop-sided planet so they're cast off to this barren rock where time creeps and slowly turns them to fertilizer. It is a hell more gruesome than what they inflicted on others, and seems unfair, it is not punishment, but the only need they can fulfill, nothing is wasted in the multi-verse. They've rendered themselves bereft of possibilities, so they scream. It will become a real annoyance as atmosphere accrues here.

"I need to go back to the eddy and immerse myself to obtain a full understanding of the forces at work here, and determine what, if any, action we might take to bring the dimension traveler to us.

"While I'm doing that, I'd like you to explore this planet. There should be other life forms. When I've learned all I can from the eddy I'll come for you."

"Okay, Honeybunch," thought the wife, and the two white poodles bounded off in opposite directions.

When the black hole tuner rejoined his mate, she was inside the planet. He followed her scent through a large carved portal shaped like the same bird of prey perched atop the planet, its head, top-center of the opening, alike in every detail.

The system accessed was impressive engineering, carried out by bustling beings similar in size and appearance to armadillos, but with serious looking mandibles dominating their heads.

Following his wife's aroma through crowds of busy tunnelers, the tuner couldn't determine whether they were oblivious to him or simply indifferent.

His wife suffered no such uncertainty. He found her in a wide stretch of tunnel, in the midst of smaller versions of tunnelers, lacking mandibles in favor of sharp little teeth. They withdrew when he approached and nuzzled her, then followed them back to the surface, crowding the portal, watching in silence long after the pair passed from sight.

A short time later, in the raggedy upper atmosphere of the lop-sided planet, a nearly invisible sphere split into a pair of large white poodles, who assumed prone positions, side by side, with an orbital speed of 27,000 kph. A small space station passed them at a distance, the flabbergasted cosmonauts began a pictorial record, exposing hundreds of frames, none of which substantiated their allegations.

"Are you noticing all the debris we're passing over?" the husband thought to his wife.

"I was just about to ask, where does it come from?"

"From the planet. The inhabitants are rapidly making it uninhabitable for themselves."

"Why would they do such a thing?"

"Maybe they fantasize travel among the stars, though they would be well advised to develop anti-gravity technology before letting their imagination run wild."

"Without anti-gravity, how did they elevate this mass of material encircling their globe?"

"Explosives."

"Naw."

Hubby said, "See all those objects bunched up and speeding away from us, down there? Every one of them needed five to seven minutes of sustained explosive thrust to get up here. The repetition created the eddy that's on the verge of spawning a black hole because it mirrored a planet breaking up and flinging pieces of itself into space."

"When will it happen?"

"Unclear, still just a probability."

"Will we be able to tell if it happens?"

"When a system's star turns black, it's a sure sign."

"Oh...What's that thing?"

"Where?"

"Back behind us, in the daylight part, the shiny thing."

"Son of a gun, we're going to see a star turn black."

"What!"

"I never got to see it happen, always came later, to tune it."

"Can you stop it?"

"You don't want to see a star turn black?"

"Can you stop it!"

"Yes, but why?"

"I don't believe this. Our children, grandchildren."

"Mister Almost a Star, manipulating us."

"I don't care about his motives. They were real and you know it. What's wrong with you?"

"I'd have to use my big hand to stop it. Last time I had to use it wiped me out took me weeks to recover."

"I'll baby you and give you lots of sex.",

"I like the way you win an argument," he said, and reached across a couple thousand miles of thin air with his big hand, tapping the rocket with a big fingernail, causing it to explode, and the tuner to lose consciousness, as the seventh portal of the dimension traveler opened before them.

The cosmonauts broke out a video camera to capture the image of an unprotected white poodle dragging a larger white poodle (also unprotected), through a hole in space that closed behind them.

Unlike the useless film snapshots, the video was perfect. After viewing it several times, the cosmonauts agreed they wished to keep their jobs, and erased it.

Dawn showed first hints of gray as Fred Hardy boxed the last of his tools and dropped the hood of his ten-year-old Dodge pick-up. He'd spent the past five hours installing a new timing chain, the type of repair he hated doing under artificial lighting, but he had a ten am meeting and contempt toward excuses. He backed the truck out of the driveway, parked on the curbless street, and spent a minute sweeping the drive with a high pressure hose, glad the temperature was mild for January

The heavy oak door was ajar, so he pushed his way through, saying, "Knock, knock."

"Come in, if your face is clean," Troll said from the next room.

He went into the bedroom. Troll sat, propped against some pillows, on the king-size, elevated waterbed, his attention focused on a new Sony Trinitron of the large persuasion. Hardy sat in an armchair catty corner to the television flashing live from Florida.

"...3....2...1...Liftoff...we have liftoff."

The decibel count grew exponentially.

Hardy looked over at Troll. "You know that's nothing but a computer controlled bomb," then looked back at the screen as the rocket exploded. "Aw, hell," Hardy groaned. "me and my big mouth."

"Shut up," said Troll.

ABOUT THE AUTHOR

Born in Lynn, Mass. Came home crying first three days of first grade, because a trio of third graders was beating me up, after school. Mom told Dad. Dad took me down in the cellar, hung a heavy bag and taught me how to punch, told me not to mess with them together, but follow until they split up and take them one at a time. I thought he was out of his mind. But I did it, I was six and used to obeying my dad. It worked great. Two days later, my mother was getting phone calls from irate moms about her little bully attacking their boys. Moved to Los Angeles and discovered reading. Got in trouble for reading Les Miserables in class, hiding it behind my open textbook.

Left college after one semester, when advised by guidance counselor (who was also English Comp. professor) that there was nothing else I could learn about writing in school. Events from that point to the present I am only at liberty to reveal under the cloak of fiction.

www.ingramcontent.com/pod-product-compliance
Lightning Source LLC
Chambersburg PA
CBHW071231130626
46555CB00004B/1942